For Tavita, my beloved mentsh
—C. K. P.
For Dad, love Pupik
—A. L.

ATHENEUM BOOKS FOR YOUNG READERS
An imprint of Simon & Schuster Children's Publishing Division
1230 Avenue of the Americas, New York, New York 10020
Text © 2021 by Caroline Kusin Pritchard
Illustrations © 2021 by Ariel Landy
Book design by Rebecca Syracuse © 2021 by Simon & Schuster, Inc.
All rights reserved, including the right of reproduction in whole or in part in any form.
ATHENEUM BOOKS FOR YOUNG READERS is a registered trademark of Simon & Schuster, Inc.
Atheneum logo is a trademark of Simon & Schuster, Inc.
For information about special discounts for bulk purchases, please contact
Simon & Schuster Special Sales at 1-866-506-1949 or business@simonandschuster.com.
The Simon & Schuster Speakers Bureau can bring authors to your live event. For more information or to book an event,
contact the Simon & Schuster Speakers Bureau at 1-866-248-3049 or visit our website at www.simonspeakers.com.
The text for this book was set in Songti TC, Minya Nouvelle, and Ogre.
The illustrations for this book were rendered digitally.
Manufactured in China
0621 SCP
First Edition
2 4 6 8 10 9 7 5 3 1
Library of Congress Cataloging-in-Publication Data
Names: Pritchard, Caroline Kusin, author. | Landy, Ariel, illustrator.
Title: Gitty and Kvetch / Caroline Kusin Pritchard ; illustrated by Ariel Landy.
Description: First edition. | New York : Atheneum Books for Young Readers, [2021] | Audience: Ages 4–8. | Audience: Grades 2–3. | Summary:
Gitty always sees the bright side of life, while her best feathered-friend, curmudgeonly Kvetch, complains constantly but when her perfect plan
goes awry, only Kvetch can raise Gitty's spirits again. Includes glossary of Yiddish words.
Identifiers: LCCN 2020026209 | ISBN 9781534478268 (hardcover) | ISBN 9781534478275 (eBook)
Subjects: CYAC: Attitude (Psychology)—Fiction. | Personality—Fiction. | Best friends—Fiction. | Friendship—Fiction. | Birds—Fiction.
Classification: LCC PZ7.1.P7695 Git 2021 | DDC [E]—dc23
LC record available at https://lccn.loc.gov/2020026209

Gitty and Kvetch

Caroline Kusin Pritchard ❀ Illustrated by Ariel Landy

Atheneum Books for Young Readers
New York   London   Toronto   Sydney   New Delhi

itty swirled, swooped, and splattered every paint from her palette until . . .

Perfect!

She raced to find Kvetch
on his favorite perch.

Kvetch,
my unflappable
friend!

Here we go....

This is the perfect day
to hang the perfect
painting in our perfect,
purple tree house.
Come with me!

Today? Gitty . . .

That's right, today!
It's PERFECT!

Haven't you heard
of the *calm* before
the storm?

And besides, I'm still
recovering from our
last adventure.

Which is exactly
why you need a
new adventure!

Gitty and Kvetch skipped Shlepped. off together.

They passed a symphony
of buzzes,

Mosquitoes.

a wave of wildflowers,

Weeds.

and the world's most
spectacularly stinky stack.

COW POOP.
It's cow poop.

Then, just as they reached the next clearing, Gitty stopped in her tracks.

Kvetch, can you even *believe* our luck? If that isn't the **brightest** . . .

Not for long.

biggest . . .

Same size as yesterday.

glowiest . . .

Oy vey.

sun I've ever seen!

A perfect sun on the perfect day to hang the perfect painting in our perfect, purple tree house.

But right in the middle of this perfect day, a cloud popped out from behind a tree.

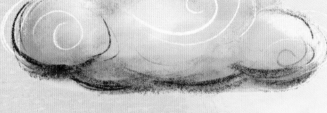

Kvetch, look! Have you ever *seen* such a stunning gray?

Rocks, grubby elephants, moldy bread . . .

And look how quickly it moves! Like a gazelle running across the savanna.

Or a lion running toward dinner.

What a joyful sign!

Of impending doom. Time to move our tuchuses!

It's the perfect cloud covering the perfect sun on the perfect day to hang the perfect painting in our perfect, purple tree house.

Then **What luck!** a wave of clouds
stretched across the sky.

Did we hit the jackpot or what? Now we get to meet the whole cloud family!

Oh yes—one big, happy mishpocheh. And look what they brought with them....

The **perfect** drizzle from the **perfect** clouds covering the **perfect** sun on the **perfect** day to hang the **perfect** . . .

Um, excuse me,
cloud family?
This is so lovely
but . . .

it's just a tiny bit
wetter than I . . .

check?

See, Kvetch?
We made it
just in time!

I'm sure everything is totally and completely . . .

Please don't say "ruined." . . .

RUINED!

Ruined?

RUINED

RUINED

RUINED!

No, not *ruined*. I bet it's just a little bit of ... shmuts. We can wipe it right off!

But for Gitty, it *was*. Her perfect painting was wet and wrecked, just like her perfect day.

A perfect
new doormat?

No! It was
supposed to be
the **perfect** way
to say . . .

you and me!

You know, on second thought,
today might just be a **magical** day
to search for **magical** treasure at the end
of the **magical**, mysterious rainbow.

KVETCH'S GLOSSARY OF
YIDDISH WORDS

Gitty: nickname for someone whose full name is "Gittel," which means "good." Pretty spot-on for my giddy best pal, don't you think?

kvetch: to complain on and on and on. I'm not sure why that name ever stuck. . . .

meshuge: totally and completely bonkers. Like most of Gitty's cuckoo ideas!

mishpocheh: the family you are born with or the family you choose. They all seem to drive me meshuge!

nosh: a delicious snack, like a worm sandwich. I'm smacking my beak just thinking about it!

oy vey: my favorite expression! I use it whenever I'm feeling overwhelmed. Which is most of the time, really.

shlep: to drag, like when Gitty drags me... on a yet another adventure. I'm a home-birdy, what can I say?

shmuts: something dirty. Yuck.

shprits: just a light spray . . . NOT a torrential downpour, Gitty!

tuchus: where I shake my tail feathers!

Yiddish: one of many Jewish languages. It includes elements of Hebrew, German, Aramaic, Slavic, and central European languages.